OLIVIA™
Star of the Show

adapted by Tina Gallo
based on the screenplay "Talent Show" written by Peggy Sarlin
illustrated by Shane L. Johnson

Simon Spotlight
New York   London   Toronto   Sydney   New Delhi

Based on the TV series OLIVIA™ as seen on Nickelodeon™

SIMON SPOTLIGHT
An imprint of Simon & Schuster Children's Publishing Division
1230 Avenue of the Americas, New York, New York 10020
OLIVIA™ Ian Falconer Ink Unlimited, Inc. and © 2014 Ian Falconer and Classic Media, LLC
All rights reserved, including the right of reproduction in whole or in part in any form.
SIMON SPOTLIGHT and colophon are registered trademarks of Simon & Schuster, Inc.
For information about special discounts for bulk purchases, please contact Simon & Schuster Special Sales at 1-866-506-1949 or business@simonandschuster.com.
Manufactured in China 1013 SCP
First Edition 10 9 8 7 6 5 4 3 2 1
ISBN 978-1-4424-9860-0
ISBN 978-1-4424-9861-7 (eBook)

"One, two, three! Eyes on me!" Mrs. Hoggenmuller sang out. "I have an enormous announcement to
make. Can anyone guess what's going to happen one week from today?"
Lots of hands shot up into the air. Everyone wanted to take a guess.
"It's going to be Tuesday again!" Francine announced.
"Yes, Francine," Mrs. Hoggenmuller said. "And what else?"
Olivia leaped to her feet and twirled. "It will be Paint-the-School-Red Day! And we'll all get big buckets of
red paint, and paint the walls red, and the floor red and . . ."

"A very colorful idea, Olivia," Mrs. Hoggenmuller said with a smile. "But here's the big news: One week from today, we're going to have a talent show!"
Olivia stopped twirling. "A talent show?" she repeated.

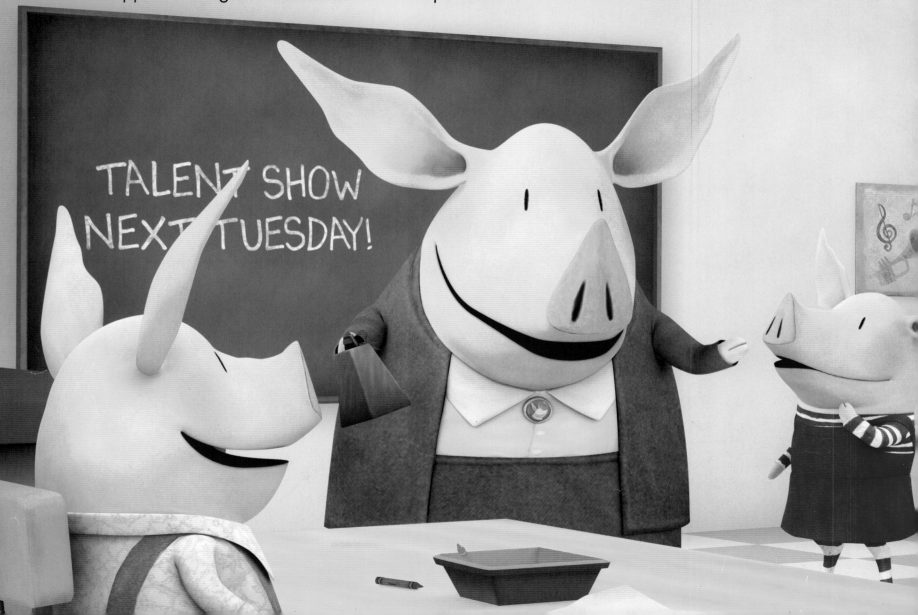

"Yes!" Mrs. Hoggenmuller answered. "All of you are invited to perform your own special talent. Sing, dance, play the kazoo—show us what you've got! Plus everyone who participates will receive a cowbell!" She held her cowbell high and gave it a hearty shake so it rang loud and clear.

Olivia sat back down in her seat. Francine leaned over and whispered to her.

"Are you going to be in the talent show, Olivia?" she asked.

"You bet!" Olivia answered. "Just as soon as I decide what my talent is. I like to do so many things. I could make a sculpture . . . or I could cook up some of my famous Super Sparkly Spaghetti . . ."

"Or maybe I could teach an animal some tricks . . ."
Olivia imagined herself standing next to a lion.

"Sit!" Olivia says, and the lion quietly sits down like a dog. "Now shake a
paw! Good lion!" Olivia says brightly as the lion offers her his paw.

"Hmm. Picking just one talent is going to be tricky," Olivia said.

Mrs. Hoggenmuller spoke up again. "Whatever you do, class, just remember to enjoy yourselves and you'll be sure to make a big bang!"

"That's it!" Olivia shouted, jumping to her feet. "I'll make a big bang!"

Back at home Olivia sat at her drum set in the living room.

"I decided to play my drums in the school talent show," Olivia told her dad. "It's my favorite way to make a big bang. If I'm going to dazzle everyone, I need to practice. A lot!"

Olivia banged out a dramatic drum solo and ended her performance with a flourish. "Ta-daaaa! How was that, Dad?" she asked.

Olivia's dad looked at her. He was holding stuffed animals over his ears. Baby William was holding stuffed animals over his ears too!

"I'm sorry, Olivia," Dad said. "Did you say something?"

Olivia smiled. "Something tells me my talent is too loud to keep quiet. Or indoors!"

Olivia took her drum set outside to practice. Her mom was busy inside the house arranging flowers when she suddenly started dancing along to the beat.
"Olivia's getting good!" she said with a smile.
Dad walked over to the window. "Really good!" he said.
Olivia finished her practice with a loud crash on the cymbals.
"You sound great, Olivia!" Dad shouted.

The day of the talent show finally arrived! Mrs. Hoggenmuller gave all
the students a pep talk backstage.
"Listen up, my talented performers! It's time to go out there and show
your friends and family what you've got."

Mrs. Hoggenmuller checked a list on her clipboard.
"Francine, you go first."
Francine gulped. "Me? *First?*"
Mrs. Hoggenmuller nodded. "First you, followed by Olivia, then Otto and Oscar, then Julian, then Daisy.
Okay, folks, it's showtime!"

"And now, here's our first performer, Francine!" Mrs. Hoggenmuller announced.

"Go, Francine!" Olivia cheered.

"I can't," Francine said. "I'm too scared."

"You're the best roller-skating princess I ever saw," Olivia told her. "You can do it. Just get out there and smile!"

Olivia gave Francine a pat on the back and a little push. Francine rolled across the stage with a frozen smile on her face. She lifted up one leg as she skated off the stage.

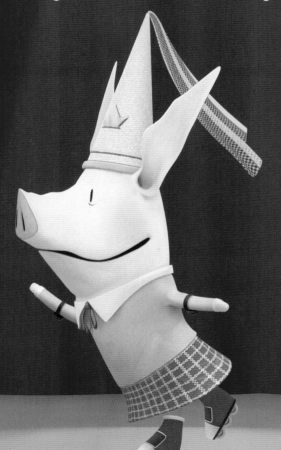

"Good job, Francine," Olivia said backstage as Francine skated past. "Um . . . Francine?"

Crash! Francine skated right into Olivia's drum set and landed headfirst in a trash can.

"I can't see!" Francine yelled from inside the can.

Olivia ran over to help. She held the trash can while Otto and Oscar each pulled on one of Francine's legs.

Meanwhile the other students went on with the show. Olivia would just have to go on later than planned.

Finally with a loud *pop!* Francine was free.

"How did I do?" she asked.

"I hope you're ready to go on, Olivia," Mrs. Hoggenmuller said a little while later. "Everyone else has performed." She looked at Olivia and gasped. "Oh no!"

Olivia stood in the middle of her broken drum set. When Francine crashed into Olivia's drums, she broke them all.

"They're broken," Olivia said sadly. "Everything except my drumsticks."

"I'm so sorry, Olivia!" Francine said. "It's all my fault."

"No, it's not, Francine," Olivia said. "You didn't mean to break them."

With a sigh Olivia dropped a broken drum into a trash can. It made a loud *bang!*

That gave Olivia an idea. She turned to Mrs. Hoggenmuller.

"Go ahead and introduce me, Mrs. Hoggenmuller," Olivia said. "Things are about to get loud!"

Mrs. Hoggenmuller announced, "And now, presenting *Olivia*!" She moved off to the side of the stage so the audience could see Olivia seated behind a set of trash cans.
It wasn't what she had planned, but Olivia was going to make the best of the situation. She gave her drumsticks a little twirl and began drumming.

Then Olivia began to sing. She was making her act up as she went along, and she was better than ever! Everyone watching her started stomping their feet in time to Olivia's beat. Olivia finished and curtsied to the audience. Everyone applauded and cheered!

When the show was over, the performers came on stage to take a final bow together. They were all holding shiny cowbells. Mrs. Hoggenmuller handed one to Olivia.
"You certainly did make a big bang!" Mrs. Hoggenmuller said.
Olivia held her cowbell high so her family could see it.

It was hard for Olivia to fall asleep that night. She sat up in bed, beating her drumsticks on her new cowbell.

"Mom, listen to this!" Olivia said.

Mom smiled. "It will sound even better in the morning, Olivia. Time for bed."

With a sigh Olivia handed her cowbell to Mom.

"You really dazzled me with your drumming today, Olivia," Mom said.

"I dazzled me, too," Olivia said with a yawn. "Good night, Mom."

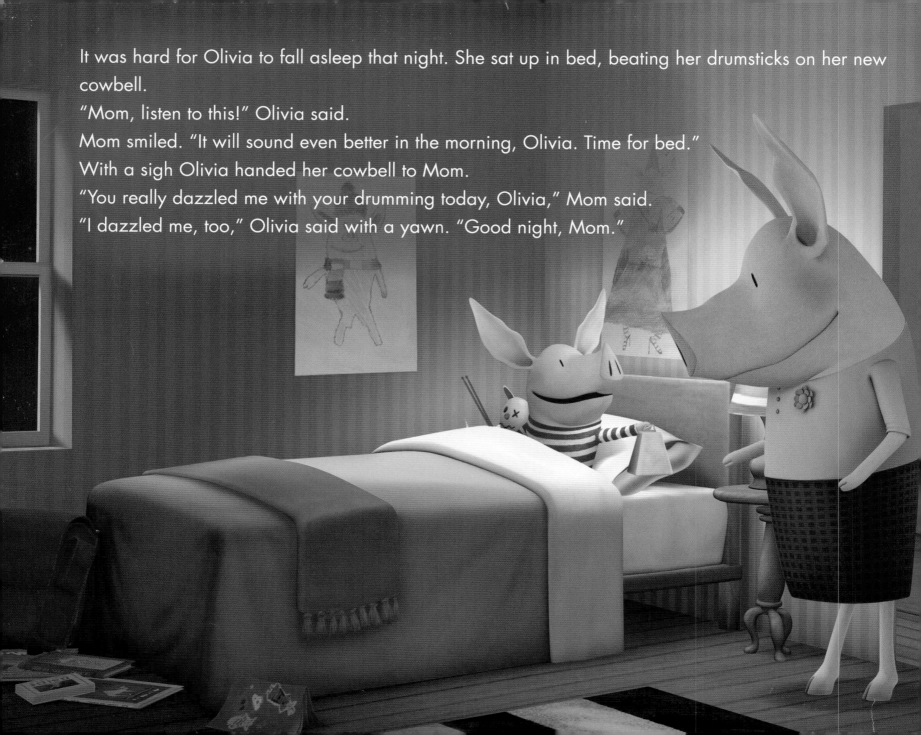